THE LIBRARY OF PHYSICAL SCIENCE™

The Structure of Atoms

Suzanne Slade

The Rosen Publishing Group's
PowerKids Press™
New York

To my children, Patrick and Christina, who give me much joy

Published in 2007 by The Rosen Publishing Group, Inc.
29 East 21st Street, New York, NY 10010

First Edition

Editors: Melissa Acevedo and Amelie von Zumbusch
Book Design: Elana Davidian
Layout Design: Ginny Chu
Photo Researcher: Gabriel Caplan

Illustrations: pp. 6, 12, 13 by Ginny Chu, p. 21 by Ginny Chu, adapted from an illustration by Tahara Anderson.
Photo Credits: Cover © Mike Agliolo/Photo Researchers, Inc.; p. 4 © Michael Pole/Corbis; p. 5 © Jon Wilson/Photo Researchers, Inc.; p. 7 © Stewart Tilger/Corbis; p. 8 © Scott Camazine/Photo Researchers, Inc.; p. 9 © Charles D. Winters/Photo Researchers, Inc.; p. 10 ©2002 PA/Topham/The Image Works; p. 11 © Erich Schrempp/Photo Researchers, Inc.; p. 14 © Corbis; pp. 15, 19 © Kenneth Eward/BioGrafx/Photo Researchers, Inc.; p. 16 © Paul A. Souders/Corbis; p. 17 © Matti Niemi/Getty Images; p. 18 © Ted Kinsman/Photo Researchers, Inc.; p. 20 © Royalty-Free/Corbis.

Library of Congress Cataloging-in-Publication Data

Slade, Suzanne.
  The structure of atoms / Suzanne Slade.— 1st ed.
      p. cm. — (Library of physical science)
  Includes index.
  ISBN 1-4042-3414-4 (library binding) — ISBN 1-4042-2161-1 (pbk.)
  1. Atoms—Juvenile literature. 2. Matter—Properties—Juvenile literature. 3. Nuclear physics—Juvenile literature. I. Title. II. Series.
QC173.16.S53 2007
539.14—dc22
                                            2005025629

Manufactured in the United States of America

Contents

What Is an Atom?

Everything in the world is formed by tiny **particles** called atoms. Atoms make up every animal, plant, and rock. Your body has **billions** of atoms. Even the air you breathe is made up of atoms.

What is the tiniest thing you can think of? Is it a grain of sand? Atoms are much smaller than grains of sand. If you smashed a single grain of sand into little bits, an atom

There are about 100,000 grains in a handful of sand.

These grains of sand are shown 100 times bigger than their real size.

would still be smaller than those pieces of sand.

Atoms are so small you cannot see them. It is impossible to measure an atom with a ruler. If you lined up one million atoms next to each other, they would measure less than 1 millimeter (.04 in)! Atoms can only be seen through special, high-powered **microscopes** used by scientists.

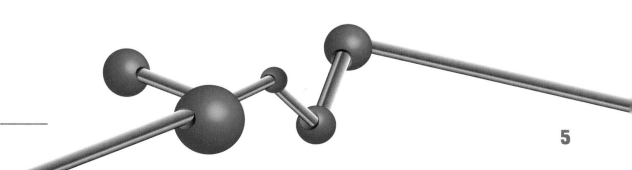

The Purpose of an Atom

Although atoms are too small to see, they have a very important job. Atoms are the basic building blocks of everything. Atoms are the smallest form of what scientists call matter. Matter is any solid, liquid, or gas that takes up space. This

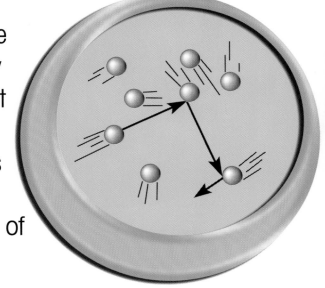

The atoms in a gas can move around freely and bump off each other, as seen above.

book, the peanut-butter sandwich you ate for lunch, and the **helium** gas inside a balloon are all matter made from tiny atoms.

Atoms are not all the same. Scientists have discovered more than 100 different kinds of atoms. How many things could you build if you had a block set with 100 different kinds of blocks? Like a set of buildings blocks, the many types of atoms can combine to create many different kinds of matter. For example, a small ant is made up of a different group of atoms than those in a tall building or a thick, chocolate milkshake. Everything is built from its own special group of atoms.

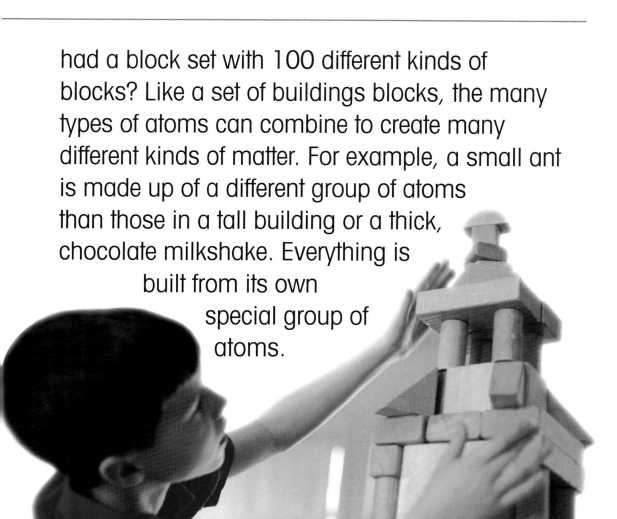

This tower is made of different blocks, just as all things are made from different atoms.

7

The Nucleus

A nucleus is found in the center of every atom. It is the heaviest part of the atom. The nucleus is made of two **subatomic** particles called protons and neutrons. Protons and neutrons are joined in the nucleus. Different types of atoms have different numbers of protons and neutrons. The number of protons in the nucleus is what makes one atom different from another.

Proton

Neutron

The nucleus of an atom is made of protons and neutrons. Electrons circle around the nucleus. The electrons are white in this computer drawing of an atom.

Selenium, above, is a gray solid with 34 protons in its atoms. If the atoms had one more proton, they would be the red liquid bromine, right.

A nucleus is about 10,000 times smaller than an atom. One of the most surprising things about an atom is that it is mostly empty. The nucleus is mostly surrounded by empty space. If you pretended that a hula hoop was an atom, its nucleus would be smaller than a grain of sand placed in the center of the hoop. Although the nucleus is small, it provides almost all the weight of an atom.

Protons

A proton is a positively charged particle. Protons are found inside the nucleus of every atom. Different types of atoms have different numbers of protons. Scientists **identify** an atom based on the number of protons it has.

Scientists also have a good idea of how an atom will act when they know its number of protons.

This man is being pulled by balloons filled with light helium gas.

Lead, shown above, is very heavy. It is used to make many things, such as glass, fireworks, and rubber.

The more protons an atom has, the more the atom weighs. A helium atom has only two protons. Helium gas is very light. It is used to make balloons float because it is lighter than air. An atom of lead has 82 protons. Lead is a heavy metal.

Neutrons

The other subatomic particle found in the nucleus is the neutron. The numbers of neutrons and protons in the nucleus are added together to find an atom's atomic mass. The neutron has no electric charge. It is **neutral**. The protons in an atom's nucleus are positively charged. Two particles with the same charge will push away from each other. Protons try to stay away from each other, just as

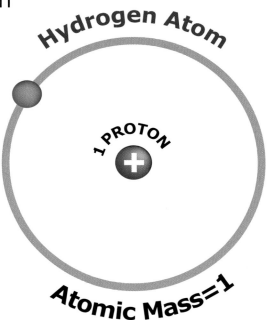

Hydrogen Atom

1 PROTON

Atomic Mass=1

Hydrogen is a colorless gas that burns easily. An atom of hydrogen has one proton and an atomic mass of one. Hydrogen atoms are the only atoms with no neutrons.

the two positive ends of magnets will push apart. Along with the **strong nuclear force**, the neutrons help keep the protons in the nucleus together. The more protons an atom has, the more neutrons it needs to help hold its nucleus together. If there are not enough neutrons, the strong nuclear force that holds the atom together could be weakened. As a result the nucleus could break apart.

Helium Atom

2 PROTONS

2 NEUTRONS

Atomic Mass=4

Helium is a light, colorless gas. A helium atom has two protons and two neutrons, so its atomic mass is four.

Electrons

The tiny particles that move around the nucleus of an atom are called electrons. Sometimes electrons join one atom to another. One atom can share or give electrons to another atom. The connection made by these electrons is called a bond.

Scientist J. J. Thomson, shown above, discovered the electron in 1897 at Cambridge University in Cambridge, England.

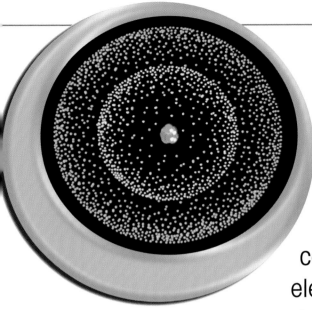

This picture shows the levels of electrons in a beryllium atom.

Electrons are arranged in levels. These levels are like the round rows people sit in around a football field. Each row holds a certain number of electrons. When one row is full, the electrons start filling the next row.

Although electrons are smaller and weigh less than protons, they have the same amount of electric charge. Atoms always have the same number of electrons and protons, so the **negative** charge from the electrons balances out the positive charge from the protons. This balance results in atoms that have no electric charge.

Electric Charges

Both protons and electrons have electric charges. Have you ever felt a shock when you touched another person? This is an example of an electric charge.

Electric charges are either positive or negative. The protons in the nucleus of an atom are positively charged. Negatively charged electrons travel around the outside of the nucleus.

The metal ball this girl is touching makes static electricity. When she touches the ball, an electric charge runs through her body and makes her hair stand on end.

The negatively charged electrons are drawn to the positively charged protons. However, the very fast speed at which electrons move around the protons keeps them from being pulled toward the protons. Have you ever ridden on a ride that traveled in a circle? The faster the ride goes, the more you feel pulled away from the center of the ride. In the same way, electrons are pulled away from protons in an atom.

This ride is called a carousel swing. The people spin around the middle of this ride just as electrons spin around the nucleus of an atom.

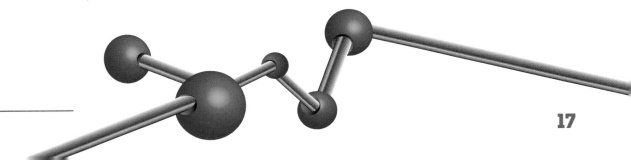

Atoms and Molecules

Atoms often connect to other atoms to form **molecules**. A small molecule may have only two atoms. For example, a molecule of **oxygen** gas is made of two oxygen atoms.

Matter that is made of only one kind of atom is called an element. Gold is an element. A gold ring is made completely of gold atoms.

Other matter has molecules that are formed from different kinds of atoms. These kinds of matter are called compounds. Water is a compound. A water molecule has two **hydrogen** atoms and one

Water covers 70% of Earth's surface. All animals and plants need water to live.

This picture of water molecules was made by a computer. The oxygen molecules are shown in red. The hydrogen molecules are clear.

oxygen atom. Many different kinds of molecules are created from the more than 100 different types of atoms in the **universe**. Molecules combine with other molecules to create everything you see in the world.

Atoms and Elements

There are as many elements as there are different kinds of atoms. Ninety-four different types of atoms occur in nature. Scientists have created 22 more kinds of atoms so far, so there are 116 different atoms and elements in all.

Elements can be solids, liquids, or gases. You breathe in oxygen and other gas elements. You might have some solid elements in your pocket. A penny is made of two elements, copper and zinc. Silver and gold are other common elements.

All the elements are shown on a chart called the periodic table. Every element

Au is the symbol for gold. The symbol comes from the first letters of *aurum*, the Latin word for gold.

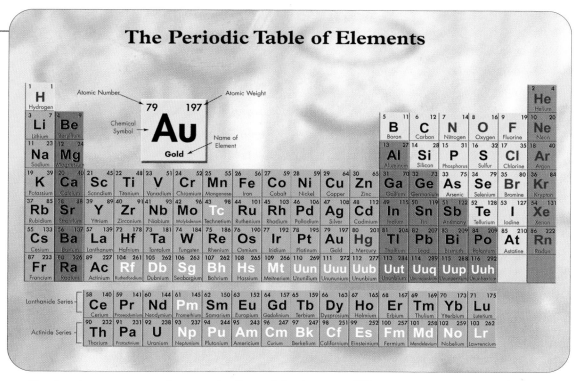

The Periodic Table of Elements

Each element on the periodic table has a different atomic number. An element's atomic number is the number of protons in one of its atoms. A gold atom has 79 protons, so gold's atomic number is 79.

has a **symbol** of one, two, or three letters. The symbol for oxygen is O. Copper's symbol is Cu. The symbol for the element ununquadium is Uuq.

Atoms in Our World

Greeks were the first to think about atoms, more than 2,000 years ago. The Greek word for the smallest piece of something, *atomos,* gave us the word "atom." Over the years people have used the same atoms in different ways. Abraham Lincoln could have breathed the oxygen atoms you are breathing in right now! Your body may even have atoms that were once part of a dinosaur!

Scientists are always learning new things about atoms. They have discovered new particles inside atoms, such as neutrinos, leptons, and quarks. These particles are too small to see, and scientists are still learning about them. There is much more one can learn about these building blocks of matter.

Glossary

billions (BIL-yunz) Thousands of millions. 1 billion is 1,000 millions.

helium (HEE-lee-um) A light, colorless gas.

hydrogen (HY-droh-jen) A colorless gas that burns easily and weighs less than any other known element.

identify (eye-DEN-tuh-fy) To tell what something is.

microscopes (MY-kruh-skohps) Instruments used to see very small things.

molecules (MAH-lih-kyoolz) Two or more atoms joined together.

negative (NEH-guh-tiv) The opposite of positive.

neutral (NOO-trul) Having no electric charge.

oxygen (OK-sih-jen) A gas that has no color, taste, or odor and is necessary for people and animals to breathe.

particles (PAR-tih-kulz) Small pieces of something.

strong nuclear force (STRONG NOO-klee-ur FORS) The force which causes the nucleus of an atom to stay together.

subatomic (sub-uh-TAH-mik) Having to do with particles that are smaller than atoms.

symbol (SIM-bul) The letter or letters that stand for an element.

universe (YOO-nih-vers) All of space.

Index

Web Sites

Due to the changing nature of Internet links, PowerKids Press has developed an online list of Web sites related to the subject of this book. This site is updated regularly. Please use this link to access the list:

www.powerkidslinks.com/lops/struct/